THE HAUNTING OF LAVENDER RAINE

THE HAUNTING OF LAVENDER RAINE

JESSICA RENWICK

Published by Starfell Press

The Haunting of Lavender Raine

Copyright 2020 @ Jessica Renwick. All rights reserved.
Contact the author at www.jessicarenwickauthor.com

ISBN (paperback) 978-1-989854-02-0
ISBN (eBook) 978-1-989854-03

Formatting by Red Umbrella Graphic Designs

Edited by Talena Winters, www.talenawinters.com
Proofread by Erin Dyrland

Printed in the United States of America, or the country of purchase.

This book or any portion thereof may not be reproduced or used in any manner whatsoever without the express written permission of the publisher except for the use of brief quotations in a book review.

OTHER WORKS BY JESSICA RENWICK

STARFELL SERIES
The Book of Chaos
The Guitar of Mayhem
The Bow of Anarchy
The Curse of the Warlock
The Song of Embers
The Star of Truth (coming 2023)

LAVENDER RAINE SERIES:
Lavender Raine and the Field of Screams
Lavender Raine and the Library of Ghosts

SHORT STORY
The Witch's Staff – Mythical Girls anthology by Celticfrog Publishing

CHAPTER ONE

"Where is it?" I touch my throat, where the necklace should be resting, but my fingers brush against smooth skin. It's gone. I point my flashlight on the ground, searching the tall grass around the stone well, but it's no use. I can't see it anywhere.

Great. Just great. First Blot, our cat, runs off into the forest. Again. Then, while searching for him out here in the dark, I lose the silver heart-shaped locket my grandma gave to my mom. The one with the old grainy photo of her and my grandpa when they were young. Why did I have to wear it tonight? Mom said I could have it in three years when I turn sixteen. That's when she thinks I will be responsible enough to have such a keepsake. I guess she has a point.

She is not going to be happy.

I let out a groan and point my flashlight up into the pine tree nearest to me. Two wide gleaming eyes stare back.

"Blot?" I squint at the creature.

It hoots softly and with a flapping of wings it takes off from the branch. Nope. Only an owl.

Okay. Breathe. What would Grandma do in a situation like this? She'd keep a cool head and think back to the last places she'd been.

It's hard to believe the necklace would fall off out here in the woods. Unless the clasp was broken. Or maybe I caught it on a branch when

I was hunting under the trees for that darn cat.

It could be at the house. Maybe I had taken it off when I got home from my painting lesson and forgot. Yes, that's it. I must have placed it in mom's jewelry box, like so many times before, to make sure it's there when she gets home from her shift at the hospital. That seems more likely.

Now what about Blot? I usually find him hanging around this old well, either sitting on the stone wall around it or prowling in the grass nearby. But tonight, he's nowhere to be seen.

I press my lips together and push aside some low-hanging branches of the pine tree. It was hot today so I'm only wearing a t-shirt and shorts, no jacket. The tree's needles scratch my forearms. But that's the least of my worries. I need to find that cat.

"Blot!" I call out, shining the flashlight over the crinkled leaves and pine cones on the forest floor. I crane my neck and look into the branches. "Here, kitty kitty."

A high-pitched mewl sounds behind me. I swing around and shine my light on the path to see the inky-black cat sitting in the grass. He swishes his tail, cocks his head, and mews again.

I breathe a sigh of relief, walk over to him, and scratch his ears. "You naughty cat. This is the second time you've run off this week, and it's only Tuesday."

He purrs and rubs his head against my hand. It's hard to stay mad at him. With his shiny coat and bright green eyes, Blot is the prettiest cat I've ever seen. He had belonged to my grandma, before she died a few weeks ago. She left him to my mom and me. Grandma used to say that as a kitten he looked like a little ink blot—hence, his name. I swallow the lump in my throat as he winds between my legs, rubbing on my calves. He must be missing her too.

Lately, Blot has been acting strange. Most nights we find him prowling around the front door, yowling to be let out. Our old farm house sits at the edge of town with the forest behind it. Whenever we open the door, we have to be careful or Blot will take off into the woods and be gone for hours.

"Let's go home, buddy." I reach to pick him up, but he lets out a low-pitched meow and dodges my hand. "What are you—"

Before I can finish, he darts down the trail into the dark.

I break into a jog, shining the flashlight

ahead of me. "Blot! Come back here! What's gotten into you?"

I go around a bend and see Blot sitting in the middle of the path, his tail twitching side to side. He looks at me with his lamp-like eyes and yowls.

"Come here, you little devil."

A chill settles over me and the hairs on my arms stand to attention. Something feels off, like there's electricity in the air. The leaves on the trees rattle above me. I look up, expecting to see a bat or, even worse, a vampire leaping from a branch.

I shake my head and laugh at myself. Clearly, I've been watching too many scary shows on TV.

When I shine my light on Blot, there's a sheet of grey fabric next to him. He's rubbing against somebody's leg! I startle and raise the beam to a young woman's face. Despite her waist-length black hair, everything seems washed out. It's as if she were in a newspaper clipping or an old black and white photo. But the strangest thing about her is how she stares right through me, unblinking, as if I'm not even here.

A shiver crawls up my spine, one vertebra at a time.

"Blot, come here."

The cat ignores me and bumps his head against the lady's shin. This breaks her from the trance, and she jerks her head toward me.

A soft voice, so quiet I'm not sure if it's in my imagination, whispers on the wind.

"Lavender."

How does she know my name? Was that even her? Her mouth didn't move! I stand frozen, willing my legs to run but they won't move. It's as if they're rooted to the ground.

The young woman reaches her hand toward me. She twitches and flickers in and out of the beam from my flashlight, quicker and more erratic with every second.

I open my mouth to scream, but my voice sticks in my throat.

She glides toward me. Right as I'm about to faint, her form dissolves, leaving behind a cloud of mist. A breeze picks up, and the haze clears. The only thing left on the trail is Blot, who is licking his front paws without a care in the world.

I gape at him, my heart hammering so hard I think I might have a heart attack. He gazes at me, and then stretches out his forepaws with a yawn, as if nothing completely crazy had just happened.

I run over to him, pick him up, and hug him tightly. He rubs his head against my chin.

Did I see a ghost? Or a witch? Maybe a zombie? I must be losing my mind! My mom believes in paranormal activity. But I don't. She's obsessed with ghost hunting shows and documentaries on haunted places. I have more sense than that.

There must be some reasonable explanation. These trails are well-used. Maybe I caught someone by surprise and she took off? It's so dark, and I was scared. I could have imagined her vanishing.

A rustling noise comes from the bushes beside the trail. I take off toward home with Blot clutched to my chest, running as fast as my legs will go.

CHAPTER TWO

I push aside a beaded necklace in mom's jewelry box and groan. Grandma's locket isn't here. Just like it wasn't ten minutes ago or any of the other times I searched the box today. I let out a breath, feeling defeated. Now what?

My long purple hair, dyed a shade that matches my name, catches my eye in the mirror of Mom's vanity table. I rake my fingers through it and glance at the digital clock on the dresser. It's two o'clock, and Mom will be home any minute from the grocery store. She has today off from her usual night shift at the hospital, and she's planning to go out with her boyfriend, Brian. She'll definitely want to wear the heart locket.

I cringe and slam the wooden box closed. Why did I have to wear that necklace yesterday? To impress Rosie, my best friend? She doesn't care about fancy jewelry. I chew the side of my cheek, gazing at the framed photo of my grandmother and Mom that sits beside the clock. In it, Grandma is young and smiling, her thick black hair swept into a ponytail behind her head. My mom, a toddler at the time, is sitting on her lap with an adorable, chubby-cheeked smile. My heart twinges.

I didn't visit Grandma near the end. I thought she had more time. About a week before she passed, my mom—who had spent that last month at Grandma's bedside in the hospital—told me the time was near. But I hated going to that depressing place and was afraid to see my grandmother sick. She was frail and no longer the bubbly, fun-loving Grandma that I was used to. My chest hurts when I think about it. I wish I hadn't been such a scaredy-cat.

And now I've lost her necklace. I grimace, thinking of how she would feel if she knew. That is, if spirits are real like my mother believes. First, I abandoned Grandma. Now this.

Speaking of ghosts, I think back to the figure in the woods last night and shudder. My mind was playing tricks on me, right?

There's a knock at the door, and I run down the stairs to answer it. Blot sits between two potted spider plants on the stand in the entryway. He lets out a curious meow.

I swing open the door, and my best friend, Rosie Kaur, greets me with a big hardcover book in her hands. Blot arches his back, looking like he's about to leap from the stand. I grab him around his belly just in time.

"Hey! What are you doing here?" The cat squirms in my arms. I try to hold him still.

"What a nice way to greet your best friend," Rosie replies with a sideways grin.

"You know what I mean. You didn't tell me you were coming over." I step aside, gripping the cat tightly as he lets out a mewl.

"I'm returning your mom's book I borrowed." Rosie comes in and grabs Blot from me with one hand. She thrusts the book at me with the other.

I take it from her and read the bold

yellow letters on the cover out loud. "Ghost Hunting—A Guide for Beginner Paranormal Investigators. Seriously, Rosie?" I raise a brow. "My mom has you wrapped up in this ghost stuff too? Or is this some light summer reading?"

Rosie rolls her eyes and tosses her elbow-length braid over her shoulder. She snuggles Blot against her chest. "Hey boy, I've missed you too." He purrs loudly. She rubs his head and turns her gaze to me. "Weird things have been happening in our house. My dad said the last owner died in there and wasn't found for weeks. I asked your mom about it, and she lent me this book."

I frown and place the book in the bookcase that sits against the wall beside the front door. The top shelves are not only filled with books about ghosts and spirits, but also titles about herbology, astrology, numerology, and a bunch of other -ology's that I have no interest in understanding. Beneath the shelves is an enclosed cabinet. It's where I imagine Mom keeps her candles and rocks and other weird trinkets. She keeps it locked, for some reason thinking I'd want to snoop. I don't. To be honest, my mom is a bit of a hippie (who else would name their daughter Lavender Azalea Raine?). And now it looks like she's roped my best friend into her weird hobbies.

"Well, good luck with the ghost hunting," I say. "Want to come in for a bit? We've got iced tea in the fridge."

"I better not." Rosie pins Blot to her side with one arm and pulls her phone from her pocket. She peers at the screen.

My face warms as I gaze at the phone longingly. Rosie is only a few months older than me, but she's had a phone for ages. My mom is dead set against me having one until I'm sixteen. Sixteen! Three more years until I catch up on technology with the rest of my class. I have a tablet I can use for messaging my friends and browsing online, but Mom checks to make sure I'm not on any social media. It's not fair. I'm not a little kid anymore. But there's no arguing with her about it. Because, you know, my social life isn't important but ghosts and star signs are.

Rosie moves her fingers quickly over the phone's screen, then looks up at me. "Warner's waiting, and he's already cranky I'm late. We're going to the skate park. Want to come?"

My mouth goes dry. I don't get along

with Warner, Rosie's latest crush. Sure, he can be funny sometimes but mostly he's just plain mean. He teased me all year about my purple hair and my mom's strange interests. Even worse, in the last week of school he 'accidentally' spilled his water bottle all over my tree-of-life painting, an art project I had been working on for weeks. It was completely destroyed, and all he did was smirk and shrug his shoulders.

Rosie started hanging out with Warner this spring, but that ended quickly after he yelled at her. They came to see me at my house before my grandma passed away. Grandma was visiting. She made us all lemonade, and Rosie accidentally spilled hers on Warner's pants. He lost his mind, screaming at her that she'd ruined his new jeans. Grandma saw the whole thing. I'd never seen her so upset before. She asked Warner to leave and later gave Rosie and I a talk about respectful friendships. After that, Rosie steered clear of him for a while. I don't know why she's hanging out with him again.

I cringe at the memory. The last thing I want to do is hang out with Warner Thompson. "No, I think I'll pass this time."

Rosie purses her lips and shifts Blot higher on her hip. He stares at me, looking as accusing as she does. "Because you don't like Warner? Look, I know he can be a jerk. But his cousin just died. He's having a hard time."

I purse my lips, thinking. Emma died a few months ago in a horrible car accident. It was awful. I can't imagine how Warner and his family must feel about something so tragic and unexpected. My grandmother's death was only a few weeks ago. It's still fresh, but at least she died a natural death and lived a full life. My chest tightens at the thought of Grandma and tears spring to my eyes. I blink them back before Rosie can see.

I shake my head. I really don't want to get into this heart-wrenching conversation with her. "No, it's not that. I lost my grandma's locket last night. I need to find it before Mom gets home, which is any minute now."

"Oh no." Her expression softens. "Do you need help looking?" She casts a nervous glance at her phone and places Blot gently on the floor. He rubs against her legs. "I could ask Warner if it's okay that I'm a bit late. I'm sure he would understand. That necklace means so much to your mom. Besides, I've been wanting to ask her some questions. I could hang around after we find it and—"

Her phone lets out a digital popping noise and vibrates loudly in her hand.

"Don't worry about it." I give her a small smile. "I wouldn't want to cause any trouble with Warner. Why don't you come over tomorrow and we'll hang out? Maybe go to the pool? Mom bought me a summer pass."

Rosie nods, looking relieved. "Sure! That'd be awesome. And maybe I can talk to her about some of the stuff going on in my house. Last night my light was flickering like crazy, and I swear I saw a figure of an old man hovering near the ceiling."

I roll my eyes. "Are you sure you weren't dreaming?"

Rosie shoves her phone in her pocket and

puts her hands on her hips. "How are you Amanda Raine's daughter? You two couldn't be any more different."

I laugh and usher her out the door. "When you grow up hearing about all this ghost stuff, but never actually see any proof, you start to wonder. Now, I have to find that necklace. Talk to you tomorrow?"

"You bet. Good luck with the locket." Rosie walks to the sidewalk, gets on her bike, and gives me a wave. "See ya later!"

"Bye!" I wave back from my spot on the front porch.

Just as she disappears around the bend, I catch sight of a black cat slinking across the porch toward the side of the house.

"Blot!" I march after him. He cowers under the rocking chair near the edge of the deck. I kneel and pull him into my arms. "Back in the house. I don't have time to worry about you running off right now."

I stand, still holding the cat. He yowls and pushes against my chest, trying to break free. "Stop it. Hold still. Why do you want to run off so badly?"

I glance out at the treeline that runs behind our house. The faint outline of a young woman wearing a long skirt is standing on the path that leads into the woods, peering at me between curtains of long black hair. My stomach jumps to my chest, and I clench my eyes closed. Blot mewls and wriggles harder, but I manage to keep hold of him.

I grit my teeth and open my eyes. The path is empty. There's nobody there.

"Jeez, Blot." I scratch his ears. He lets out

a disgruntled meow, going limp in my arms. "I think I've been listening to my mom and Rosie too much. If I'm not careful, I'm going to actually start believing in that ghostly nonsense."

CHAPTER THREE

I am sitting on the couch in the living room reading my favourite book, the third Harry Potter, when I hear Mom call my name from upstairs. I sigh and set the book on the coffee table. I knew this was going to happen. The necklace is still missing, and I'm starting to worry that I did lose it in the woods.

"Lavender!" she calls again, her voice frantic.

I glance at the clock on the table beside me. 6:50. Brian should be here in ten minutes to pick her up. She always does this, wasting time until the last minute to get ready. And he always waits patiently for her. The man is a saint.

I sigh and head up the stairs. "Coming!"

When I enter her bedroom, Mom has her curling iron in one hand and is rifling through her jewelry box with the other. She's wearing a pretty floral top but is still in her plaid pajama pants. Her long brown hair is half curled, the other half clipped on top of her head. As usual, she is nowhere near ready.

"What's up?" I know exactly what's up, but I lean against the door frame and try to look casual.

She glances at me with a worried expression. "Lavender, love, have you seen your grandma's locket? I must have left it laying around somewhere."

Guilt settles over me like a cloak of shame. My cheeks grow warm, but I can't bring myself to tell her the truth. I'll look in the woods again. It was dark when I looked last night, I probably missed it.

"No, I haven't seen it." I cringe at the lie. But it's only a fib, right? There's no point in upsetting her. Once the locket is found, she'll forget it was ever gone. Mom is constantly losing things—her keys, her earrings, even her wallet. It's not like it's unusual for something to be misplaced around here. The missing objects always find their way back eventually.

Mom frowns and shakes her head, loosening one of the clips. A lock of hair falls over her face. She brushes it aside. "I was really hoping to wear the locket tonight. Brian and I are going to that new restaurant downtown. You know, the one that uses only locally grown produce. I want to look nice."

I walk over to her and take the curling iron from her hand. "You do look nice. I'll help you finish your hair. Why don't you wear that silver necklace with the rose pendant? It matches your shirt."

Mom's eyes light up, and she turns to the wooden box on her vanity table. "You're right. The rose necklace will match perfectly. What would I do without you?"

I unclip her hair and twist a strand around the curling iron. She searches the jewelry box for the right necklace. For a moment, we're quiet and I concentrate on creating the perfect curls to frame her freckled cheeks.

Mom breaks the silence, looking at me in the mirror with a kind smile. "You know,

Lavender, your grandmother would be really proud of you. You've got such a good head on your shoulders."

Biting my tongue, I think of the lie I told her earlier. What would Grandma think of that? I push the thought from my mind and nod towards the pile of books on her cluttered nightstand.

"According to all that crazy ghost stuff you read, Grandma's probably watching us right now." I tease her with a dry grin.

She casts me a puzzled look in the mirror. "Only spirits with unfinished business stick around here on Earth. What would she possibly have to make her stay?"

I bite my lip to stop from laughing. "I was joking. You know I don't believe—"

There's a rap at the door downstairs, saving me from another awkward conversation about the spirit world. It must be Brian, right on time.

I pass Mom the curling iron. "I'll let him in. You finish getting ready."

"Thanks, love." Mom gives me a grateful look and then peers at her reflection. "I'll only be a few minutes."

I trot down the stairs to the front door. Blot is pacing in front of it, waiting for it to open so he can bolt.

I pick him up and tuck him into the crook of my arm. "Not tonight, buddy."

With my free hand, I open the door and let Brian in. He greets me warmly, as he always does. I've liked Brian from the moment Mom introduced us. We first met when she took us for ice cream a few months ago. He bought me a waffle cone with all the good sprinkles and chocolate syrup, proving how awesome he is. And with his salt and pepper hair and warm brown eyes, he gives off an aura of calm kindness.

Wait, an aura? Now I sound like Mom again. What I mean to say is, he's a nice guy.

He closes the door behind him and smiles. "Your mom ready? I'm really looking forward to trying the grass-fed steak at this new restaurant."

I set the struggling Blot on the floor, who gives me a disgruntled mewl. He sits and stares at the door, swishing his tail back and forth.

"Just about. She might beat her last time. What was she, thirty minutes late?"

Brian chuckles and rubs his chin. "I think it was twenty-seven minutes. But I really don't mind. She's worth the wait."

We make small talk for a few moments,

and soon Mom comes down and wraps a flowy blue shawl around her shoulders. She grabs her purse and gives Brian a peck on the cheek.

She turns to me and gives me a hug. "Alright, love. We plan to see a movie after dinner, so don't wait up. I doubt I'll be home before midnight."

"See you later, Lavender." Brian nods.

"Bye." I block Blot with my leg so he can't run out the door, and Mom and Brian leave. I turn the locks and rub the cat's ears. "Door's closed, buddy. What do you say, should we watch a movie?"

Blot cocks his head and gives me an intense stare.

"No, we're not going outside. You lost that privilege." I give him a sideways look. "I promise we won't watch Pet Semetary again.

What about Hocus Pocus? I think there's a black cat in that one, just like you."

Suddenly, Blot yowls and dashes between my legs. He hightails it into the kitchen and leaps onto the counter, knocking Mom's potted cactus to the floor. He presses against the window above the sink, staring out at the trees.

"What are you doing?" I stomp after him. Thankfully the pot didn't break, but there's dirt all over the floor. I'll need to clean the mess and put the cactus back in place—hopefully the roots aren't too damaged. "Ugh, Blot! What's gotten into you lately?"

I reach to grab him, but stop when I look out the window. That flickering lady is out there again, standing on the back lawn. Mist swirls around her, but I can see her clearly in the dusky light. She's wearing that same long skirt and ruffled blouse. Her hair hangs over her face like a black sheet, but she's staring right at me. I can feel it.

Blot yowls and bats at the window with his front paws.

I close my eyes and shake my head, hoping she'll be gone when I open them. But she's not. She's still there, grainy and washed out, staring at the house. My stomach churns.

The creepy lady raises her arm and jerks her hand, beckoning me to join her.

No way! I pull Blot from the window sill and shove him under my arm. My heart races as I close the curtains, then rush up the stairs to my bedroom. Blot wriggles free, but I slam the door of my room so he can't get out.

Crouching low, I make my way to my window and peek out at the lawn. The woman is now at the edge of the forest. She appears to be floating, not walking, as she moves into the trees.

There's no way this is my imagination.

I pull my tablet from my nightstand, bring up my messaging app, and find Rosie's name at the top.

You're not going to believe this, I type frantically. Can you come over? Like, right now?

CHAPTER FOUR

A few hours later, I'm sprawled across the fluffy purple rug on the hardwood floor of my bedroom. Rosie lays next to me, pouring over some of my mom's crazy books. Blot is curled up on my bed, purring in his sleep.

"Okay, so you said she has scraggly black hair and wears a long skirt?" Rosie flips a page of the book in front of her.

I scrunch my nose, hardly believing that I'm actually going along with this. "Yeah. I couldn't see her face very well, but she looks young. Maybe twenty?"

Rosie jerks her head and stares at me. "Could she be a teenager? Like fifteen or sixteen?"

"I guess so. Why?"

She raises her eyebrows. "Warner's cousin, Emma. She was a few grades ahead of us. She had hair like that, dark and really long. It almost reached her butt. It could be her. Maybe she has some unfinished business, like your mom said."

"But why would she bother me? I hardly even knew her." I'd seen her in the hallways at school, but I'd never talked to her.

Rosie taps a purple-polished fingernail on her chin, lost in thought. "Well, maybe it has to do with the woods? Her house is smack in the middle of town. If she needs something from the forest, you might be her only connection."

"Maybe."

"What we need is a way to talk to her," Rosie says. "A way to find out what she wants. We could help her, and then she'd be ready to move on."

"Move on where?" I ask.

Rosie shrugs. "To wherever it is ghosts go. Heaven, I guess. The light."

"You've been watching way too much Ghost Whisperer."

She ignores me and points to the page in front of her. It has a picture of a board with letters and numbers printed on it. "It says here, we can talk to spirits with a Ouija board."

I shake my head. "No way. I've listened to my mother enough to know those things can be trouble."

"I thought you didn't believe in any of this." Rosie smirks.

I sigh and twirl a strand of my lavender hair around my forefinger. "I don't. But I saw something. And if even part of this stuff is true, I don't want to risk summoning some sort of demon into my house."

Rosie laughs and jabs her finger at the book. "We won't summon a demon. There are clear directions right here on how to do it properly. As long as we're firm and clear that we have good intentions, the door won't open to anything evil." She pauses, her jaw set in determination. "Your mom must have a Ouija board around here somewhere."

"Of course she does. But I have no idea where, and I don't think she'd tell me." I tuck the lock of hair behind my ear and get to my feet. "Besides, I don't want to tell her about this. She'd think I'm getting interested in this stuff, and then she'd never let it drop. Maybe we should let this ghost sort her business out by herself."

Rosie stands and lays the open book on my bed. "Do you want this ghost to keep pestering you? What do you think will happen if your mom sees her?"

I rub my forehead. She has a point. I need to go into the woods again to look for Grandma's necklace. Even if it is silly, I have to admit that I'm terrified of running into that ghost, or whatever she is. And if Mom sees her, we'll be on some wild ghost hunting mission. She'd probably film it and put it on YouTube. I shudder. No, Rosie's right. We need to get rid of this spirit.

"Okay," I relent. "You win. We'll try to contact her. But I'm not sure where my mom keeps that Ouija board. She hasn't used it for years." I pause, thinking of my grandmother again. "And while we're searching for it, keep an eye out for my grandma's locket. I still haven't found it."

Rosie pats my arm. "Don't worry. It's got to be here somewhere. Maybe we'll score and find both it and the Ouija board."

"I hope so." I glance at the clock on my nightstand. "We've got about two hours before Mom gets home. Let's get moving."

A few hours later, I'm still awake, waiting for Mom. Feeling defeated, I'm sitting on the couch with Blot on my lap. I stare at the TV and mindlessly skim shows for something good.

Rosie and I looked everywhere, but we didn't find the Ouija board or the locket. What am I going to do?

Mom comes in the front door and looks surprised when she sees me. "Oh, hi, love. What are you doing up?" She takes off her shawl and hangs it along with her purse on the coat hook by door.

I shrug and run my hand over Blot's sleek fur. He lets out a cute little squeak but doesn't wake. "Can't sleep. How was your date?"

"Oh, it was wonderful! That restaurant is fantastic. They have the best sweet potato fries I've ever had." Mom pauses at the entry to the kitchen. "Want some tea? I'm going to have some chamomile to help settle me down for bed."

"Sure," I reply. "Thanks."

I switch off the TV, and a few minutes later Mom comes in and hands me a steaming mug. She sits on the couch next to me.

"Now, what's bothering you tonight?"

I warm my hands on the cup, grateful for the comfort it provides. Where do I even start? There's a creepy ghost stalking me? Oh, and I've lost your precious necklace?

I swallow. "I miss Grandma, that's all."

Mom pats my knee. "Oh, love, I do too. It'll get easier with time, but there will always be a part of you that misses her. She'll always be there, in your heart."

Mom is big on this sentimental stuff. I've never been any good at it.

I take a sip of my tea and then cradle the mug in my lap. "Well, while we're on the topic. Do you think there's any way we could—um—

contact her?"

Mom frowns and sets her tea on the coffee table. She wipes her hands on her skirt. "What do you mean?"

I clear my throat. It's worth a try. "Well, I was reading in one of your books about Ouija boards and talking to our passed loved ones."

"No," she shakes her head. "That's not safe, love. You can't control what you would invite into our home. Those things can open doors to worlds that you aren't even aware exist. Besides, I'm certain Grandma has passed over to the light. She told me she was ready before she went."

"How can you be sure?"

Mom stares at me for a moment. "I can't. But I haven't seen her around here, have you?"

"No," I reply. "I wish I could talk to her.

That's all."

Mom is quiet for a minute. She slides her gaze to the bookshelf beside the entryway. For a moment, her eyebrows crease as she stares at the locked bottom door.

My pulse races. That's it. That's where the Ouija board is.

She pats my leg again with a look of concern. "Promise me you won't try to contact Grandma. She's at peace on the other side."

She probably wouldn't be if she knew about the lost locket. I push the thought to the back of my mind. I'll have to worry about that tomorrow.

"I promise I won't try to contact Grandma." Guilt settles into the pit of my stomach. But I'm not lying. I'm not going to try to contact Grandma—just Emma, or whatever ghost it is that's been bothering me. Besides, it's not like spirits actually exist, right? I'm only doing this to prove to Rosie, and to myself, that it's merely some creepy lady who goes for walks in the woods.

Mom gives me a warm smile and picks up her tea. "Good. Those Ouija boards can be finicky. We wouldn't want any uninvited spirits hanging around."

I gulp and take another sip of tea. If she only knew.

CHAPTER FIVE

I wait all day for Mom to leave for her night shift. My stomach is tight with a ball of nervous energy settled into the pit of it. It's evening now, and I'm sitting on the couch flipping through a garden magazine with Blot snoozing next to me. I don't really see the pages though; I'm too busy with my own thoughts.

Mom and I had a nice afternoon in our garden, pulling weeds and laughing over some old stories about Grandma. How she once planted onions upside down, thinking the roots were the leafy bits at the top. She managed to dig them up and save them once she realized her mistake. And about how she had random patches of dill weed growing in the strangest places in her yard. Once, while preparing to can pickles, I couldn't find the dill in her garden. She reminded me that it was growing behind the compost bin that year. Sure enough, she was right. Somehow, despite all her mishaps, her garden always flourished. Grandma had a way with plants, and animals too.

This talk made me miss her even more. What if Mom's right? Sure, she might be at peace on the other side. But if that's true, how would she be feeling about me abandoning her in that hospital bed during those last days of her life? I didn't get to say a proper goodbye or tell her how much I loved her. And does she know

I lost her necklace? One of her most precious possessions—besides Blot—that she left us? My stomach hurts thinking about it.

Mom appears at the door, wearing her navy-blue scrubs patterned with yellow smiley faces. "All right, love. I'm off for another shift in the ER." She digs through her purse and pulls out her keys. "Hopefully it's a quiet night. What time is Rosie coming over?"

I place the magazine on the coffee table. "Should be any time. There's a new series on Netflix we want to start, so hopefully she'll get here soon." I run my fingers through my hair and examine its purple tips, hoping Mom doesn't catch the lie.

"Make sure to clean up if you make popcorn." Mom swings the door open and I place my hand on Blot's back in case he decides to run for it. He opens one eye and sniffs but makes no attempt to move from his comfy spot.

Mom glances at me over her shoulder and bites her lip. "When you have time, could you take a look in your room for Grandma's necklace? I know you wouldn't steal it, but things end up in weird spots in this house. I still can't find it."

My stomach twists. I can't meet her eye. "Sure. I'll take a look."

"Thanks, dear. Love you."

"Love you too."

She leaves and I hold my breath, waiting. Her car rumbles as it backs out of the driveway.

I dash to the bookcase, then squat and check the door on the bottom shelf. Sure enough, it's locked. If I were Mom, where would I hide that key?

Just as I'm about to head into the kitchen to search the junk drawer, there's a knock at the door. I glance at the couch. Blot stretches out his forepaws and yawns sleepily. He's not going anywhere.

I open the door and Rosie slips inside, her face lit up with excitement.

"I brought some candles and herbs," she says in a hushed voice, as if my mom or the ghost is listening in. "I read that burning cinnamon will sweeten the air and entice the ghost to come forward."

I stare at her. "That's ridiculous. And you don't need to whisper, Mom left. I can't get this cabinet door open, anyways." I tap it with my foot.

Rosie grins, puts down her bag, and pulls a bobby pin from the messy bun on top of her head. Within seconds she has the pin bent into an L-shape, and she kneels in front of the bookcase.

"No problem, these locks are easy to break into." She closes one eye and squints with the other as she inserts the bobby pin into the lock. After a few seconds of twisting, she pulls the handle and the door opens.

My jaw drops. "Where did you learn that?"

"Warner." Rosie smirks and peers inside the cabinet. "Oh, wow."

"What?" I crouch beside her.

She pulls out a big wooden box and places it on her lap. She blows the dust from the top and lifts the lid. Inside lay six white and purple candles, a white cloth, a small scorched copper bowl, a bag of herbs, and a folded piece of paper. Underneath these materials sits a board with ornate letters and numbers carved into the wood. I gulp—a Ouija board.

Rosie looks at me, her eyes shining with excitement. "I'd say your mom has done this before."

I shift uncomfortably, gazing at the box's contents. The light above us flickers. Blot yowls, and I look up to see him perched at the edge of the couch, staring at us with unblinking eyes.

My mouth goes dry. "I'm not sure if this is a good idea."

Rosie stands, the box clutched in her arms. "I thought you didn't believe in this stuff," she teases. She climbs the stairs toward my bedroom. Blot bounds from the couch and follows her.

She looks over her shoulder at me. "Got a

lighter? Let's get this started."

I swallow and head into the kitchen to grab a lighter from the shelf above the sink. The light above the table flashes on and off. My heart leaps to my throat.

What have I gotten myself into?

CHAPTER SIX

The candles flicker as I sit cross-legged on my bedroom floor. Rosie sits across from me, reading the paper that was inside the wooden box. She's already placed the candles in a circle, with the copper bowl filled with herbs. The Ouija board sits in the middle. Blot is laying on the bed watching us, his tail swishing from side to side.

With the lights turned out and the blinds closed, the candles cast distorted shadows on the walls. Thunder claps in the distance, and rain begins to patter on the roof. A storm is rolling in, which does nothing to help my nerves.

I wind a lock of hair around my finger, anxiously watching Rosie. I try to swallow my fear. None of this paranormal stuff is real, I remind myself. This isn't going to work. Is it?

"According to this," Rosie waves the paper in my direction, "we need to light the herbs and then focus on the spirit we are trying to contact while we say the chant they have written here. Replace the word Spirit with Emma."

"Who wrote that?" I ask.

Rosie shrugs and shakes the paper at me. "I don't know. Your mom?"

I take the paper from her. I don't recognize the handwriting. The letters are delicate and flow daintily together. It's definitely not my mom's messy scrawl.

The sound of thunder crashes again, this time louder.

I shake my head. "Nope, not hers." I pause, frowning at the chant written on the page. "This is weird. I don't like it."

Rosie picks up the copper bowl and the lighter. With a flick of her fingers, she lights the bowl's contents and sets it back beside the Ouija board. "Stop worrying so much. We're contacting Emma to help her. And to get her off your back."

I nod, relenting. If by some long shot this does work, Emma—or whoever she is—will go to the light. Or whatever. Then, I'll be able to search the woods in peace for Grandma's necklace. I set my jaw. It will be worth it if I can find that locket.

"Now, place your fingers on the planchette,"

Rosie says.

"The what?"

She sighs. "The piece that moves."

"Oh, okay." I put the piece of paper face-up beside the Ouija board, then place my fingers on the tear drop shaped piece of loose wood that sits on top of it.

Rosie sets her fingers next to mine and stares at me from across the circle, the candlelight dancing across her. "Ready?"

I nod and she closes her eyes. Apparently, she memorized the chant. I did not. She starts reciting it. I join in, reading the words on the paper. The sound of rain pounding on the roof gets louder, almost drowning out our voices.

"Beloved Emma, we seek your guidance. We ask that you commune with us and move among us."

We finish, and nothing happens.

Rosie peeks one of her eyes open. "You didn't close your eyes!"

"I didn't know we had to," I reply. "How could I memorize—"

Lightning cracks, lighting up the room for a split second. A moment later, thunder booms and the candles wink out. The flame in the copper bowl flares higher, casting a menacing orange glow over the circle. Blot growls, and I dart my gaze to him. He's prowling across my bed, the hair on his back standing on end.

A sharp cold settles deep into my bones. I shiver and stare at Rosie. Her face is drawn, and she stares at me with wide eyes.

The planchette under our fingers begins to move.

My heart leaps to my throat. "Are you

doing that?"

"Ssh!" Rosie hisses, her gaze now glued to the board.

My stomach churns as the planchette slides from letter to letter.

L - O - C - K - E - T.

I resist the urge to pull my fingers away. It has to be Rosie doing it. "Rosie—"

She shoots me a dark look, and I close my mouth. The flame in the bowl whooshes upwards.

W . . . I hold my breath. W? What could that mean?

Suddenly, Blot lets out an ear-splitting yowl. He leaps off the bed and across the circle, knocking over the candles. Luckily, he misses the blazing bowl.

I pull my hands from the board to try and

grab him, but I'm too late. He springs onto my dresser and pushes on the window behind it. Somehow, the blinds shoot up and lightning fills the sky. The ghostly girl's form flashes in the window—staring straight at us.

I shriek, jump to my feet, and flick on the light switch beside the door. I whirl to the window, and the ghost is gone.

"Lavender!" Rosie's eyes are round as tennis balls.

"No. No way, Rosie. We're done with this." I march to the circle and blow out the fire in the copper bowl, which is now a tiny flame.

Despite the fear still tingling in my spine, I walk over to the window, grab Blot, and cuddle him to my chest. I can't decide if I should be angry with him or thank him for chasing off the ghost. I decide on the latter and stroke his soft fur. He relaxes in my arms and begins to purr.

Rosie gets to her feet, grinning. "She knows about your locket! It's too bad Blot freaked out and ran her off, but I think we're a step closer to figuring this out. Let's try again, this time we'll lock Blot out of the room."

I hold Blot tighter, causing him to squirm, and glare at her. "Are you kidding me? There's absolutely no way we're doing that again."

"But—"

"No way." I stomp from the room, still hugging the wiggling cat, afraid to let go.

CHAPTER SEVEN

I'm sitting on the couch in the living room with Blot still hugged in my arms. I try to calm my racing heart. It's still raining, but the storm has passed by. Thunder sounds in the distance, quieter than before.

What happened upstairs? My brain is numb. Did I really see Emma in the window, or was my imagination running wild because of the storm and that stupid Ouija board?

Blot purrs when Rosie enters the room, carrying two steaming cups of tea.

"Here." She sits in the arm chair beside the couch and places both mugs on the coffee table. "This might help calm your nerves. Are you okay?"

"Thanks. And I don't know." I let go of Blot. He curls up beside me and begins to lick his paws. I pull my knees to my chest and rest my chin on them. "Did you see her too? Or am I nuts?"

Rosie nods, a smile twisting on her lips. "I saw her. Clear as day. She was nothing like the man I saw hovering near my ceiling. He was faint, barely visible. She was—well, she was clearly there!"

I groan and close my eyes. "What does she want?"

"She knows something about your grandma's necklace. I wish Blot hadn't scared her off. We didn't get the full message." Rosie grins gleefully as she picks up her tea. "This is so cool. We have a real-life paranormal mystery on our hands."

"But why would she care about my grandma's necklace?" I ask. "She hardly even knew me, much less my grandma."

Rosie shrugs and takes a sip of the steaming liquid in her cup. "Maybe it's not your grandma's. What if Emma had a locket too? Or maybe she's here on other business, but saw the necklace and is trying to help you too? We should do some digging to find out."

I give her a sidelong look. This is not how I want to spend my summer. I want to read books, ride my bike, and lay by the pool. The last thing I want is a ghost hunting mission. I didn't even entertain the thought that spirits were real until tonight.

Rosie cocks her head and gives me a knowing look. "She isn't going to leave you alone until this is resolved. Besides that, won't it be worth it if we find your grandma's locket?"

I frown, but give her a nod. "I guess so. But what do we do next?"

"We could get the Ouija board out—"

"No," I cut her off. "I'm not doing that again. I'm still freaked out."

Rosie places her tea on the coffee table and shrugs. "Okay. If you don't want to, that's fine. I get it. That was pretty scary. But it was cool too."

I breathe a sigh of relief. "You know, I bet we're the only two kids in our class who have seen a real ghost."

Rosie grins. "I bet Aubrey and all those

snobby friends of hers will be so jealous. I wonder if there's a way to ask Emma to haunt her? She could give her a little scare."

I giggle and lower my legs to the floor. "Too far, Rosie. Way too far."

Rosie curls her feet on the arm chair. "Come on, after all the crap she put us through last year, she deserves a spook. Remember how she drew that awful picture of you picking your nose and gave it to Brock? She knew you had a crush on him."

Feeling better, I pick up my tea and warm my hands around the mug. I shake my head, smiling at the thought of the meanest girl in our class getting a visit from a ghost. "No. I don't think that's how ghosts work anyways. We can't just request their haunting services."

Rosie's smile fades. "But seriously, what are

we going to do next?"

"You're the expert. I've never read any of my mom's crazy books."

"I know you're not a fan of him," she says, giving me a nervous look. "But I think we should talk to Warner. He might know why Emma is still hanging around and what she wants. And what she meant by mentioning the locket."

My spine stiffens at his name, but she has a point. He could help. "Do you think he'd believe us?"

As if on cue, Rosie's phone pings. She fishes it from her pocket and stares at the screen. Colour blushes over her cheeks. "Speak of the devil."

It seems like lately Warner is always texting her. Every time we're together, he interrupts with some sort of demand. I hate how she caters to him.

"What does he want?" I ask.

Rosie presses her lips together and won't meet my eye. "Oh, he's just worried. He texted half an hour ago, and I didn't reply. He wants to meet up."

I look at the clock. "It's nine o'clock. Aren't you supposed to be home soon?"

She shrugs and stands from the chair. "I told my mom we were watching movies and I might be late."

"My mom will never go along with that." I frown. "And neither will I."

"She won't ask." Rosie steps to the entryway and looks over her shoulder at me. "Are you okay here alone?"

I glance outside at the pouring rain. Mom won't be home until late, she doesn't get off her shift until three o'clock in the morning. But I can't be a baby. I'm safe inside, and I've got Blot to keep me company.

"I'm fine. I've got Blot to protect me." I give her a confident smile. "We'll watch something on Disney to distract us."

Rosie smirks. "No ghost movies?"

"No way." I stroke Blot's back, and he arches into my hand.

"Okay. Text me later if you can't sleep." She goes to the door and puts on her shoes. "I'll talk to Warner about Emma. Maybe we should meet with him tomorrow so you can talk to him too?"

"Okay," I reply, feeling queasy at the thought of asking him about his dead cousin. But Rosie knows him better than I do and if she thinks it's a good idea, I'll have to trust her. "Talk to you later. Have fun."

"Later!" She gives a little wave and closes the door behind her, leaving Blot and I alone.

I flick on the TV and skim through the shows for kids. I need something light and funny to distract me. Blot mews and bumps me with his head. I pull him in close to my side. Thunder claps again in the distance, and I shrink further into the squishy couch cushions, hoping that I won't see Emma again tonight.

CHAPTER EIGHT

I crack my eyes open. Emma is leaning over me, empty black sockets where her eyes should be. Her hair hangs in matted clumps, nearly touching my face. I squirm, my heart pounding in my chest, and her pale lips part as if she's about to speak.

The front door slams shut, and I bolt upright, woken from my nightmare. Blot hisses and pounces from his spot beside me to the floor. Emma's gone. It was only a dream.

I flick on the lamp on the table beside the

sofa and rub my aching neck. Sleeping on this worn old couch is not good for anybody's spine.

My mom's voice floats into the room. "Lavender? What are you doing up? It's five in the morning."

I squint towards the door. Mom hangs up her rain jacket and kicks off her shoes.

"I must have fallen asleep. Blot and I were watching a movie," I reply. The TV screen is paused on a cartoon. I grab the remote from the coffee table and turn it off. "What are you doing home so late?"

She bustles into the living room and sits on the end of the couch. "Brian took me out for coffee after work. Such a love, getting up in the middle of the night to see me for an hour or two."

Her cheeks are flushed and her eyes bright.

She's excited about something.

"Oh, that's great. Very nice of him." I rub my eyes and shake my head, trying to clear my foggy brain. "You look happy."

She smiles even wider and giggles. "Well, he did have a surprise for me. For us, actually."

This grabs my attention. She's acting like a kid at Christmas. What's going on?

"What is it?"

"We're going on a trip." She wraps her arm around me in a hug. "Brian's taking us to Hawaii!"

"What?" I'm fully awake now. We haven't been on a trip for ages, not since I was five or six when we went to Disneyland with Grandma. "Seriously?"

Mom lets out a gleeful squeal. "Yes! We're going to Maui in November. It's going to be amazing. He's going to e-mail me some information about the resort and we can pick out some fun activities to do."

I push all thoughts of the ghost stuff from my mind. I don't want to distract Mom from this happy news, and I could use something fun to focus on too.

"We should make a list of what to pack," I say.

Mom blows through her lips and laughs. "Lavender, it's only July. We have ages to worry about that. But maybe we should think about finding a pet sitter for Blot. Do you think Rosie would be up for it?"

I pause, deflating a little at the thought of Rosie. I wonder how her visit with Warner went.

"Probably," I reply. "I'll ask her tomorrow. Err, today I mean."

"What are you two up to today?" Mom asks.

I wrinkle my nose. "She wants me to do something with her and Warner. She really wants me to like him."

Mom pats my leg and gives me a soft look. "And you really don't like him, do you?" It was more of a statement than a question.

I shake my head and scowl. "No, I don't. He's rude and mean. He's always annoyed with her for hanging out with me, and texts her constantly when we're together. And she ditches me when he asks her to hang out with him instead. I feel like he's taking her away from me."

Mom wrinkles her brow. "Don't give up on her, love. He's jealous of how close you two are. He's dealing with a lot, with the death of his cousin and all, but it's no excuse for him to be controlling and demanding. Try not to push her away, she may need you more than you think."

"Well I hope she realizes what he's doing soon. She could do so much better than him." I cross my arms. "She was here last night hanging out until he beckoned, then she rushed off to make him happy."

Mom gives me a sad smile. "Just stick by her, Lavender. Show her you're a true friend and will be there for her no matter what." She pauses. "You know, your grandma was with a man like that once."

"Really?" That didn't sound like Grandma. She was so strong and independent. And while I never met my Grandpa (he passed away before I was born), Mom always talked so lovingly about him. She said he treated her and Grandma like gold. In all of her childhood pictures they look like the happiest family.

Mom nods her head. "Not Grandpa. It was her boyfriend before him. That guy—he tried to break-up her friendships and relationships with her family. I don't know for sure, but there was a rumour that he hit her once. Luckily, she ended it before she married him. Could you imagine?" She paused. "Your grandma's life would have been so different if she'd stayed with that awful man and hadn't met Grandpa. You and I wouldn't even exist."

I let this new information swirl around my head. I had no idea Grandma had been through all that. It made me respect her even more, knowing she had the courage to stand up to somebody like that. Maybe if I share this with Rosie, she'll realize what a jerk Warner is.

"Anyways, love." Mom gets to her feet and kisses me on top of my head. "I need some sleep. And you look like you could use a few hours too."

I yawn in reply and flop back onto the couch.

"Why don't you go upstairs to your bed?"

Emma's creepy face in the window flashes through my mind.

"I'm too lazy. I only need another hour or two, I'll stay here."

Mom shrugs. "Suit yourself. Sleep tight." She climbs the stairs to her bedroom.

Blot leaps on top of me and curls up on my stomach. He stares at me with his big green eyes and mews.

"Keep a watch out for Emma." I tell him. I close my eyes and hope for happy dreams of Hawaii instead of nightmares about ghosts.

CHAPTER NINE

The next day, I meet Rosie and Warner at the ice cream shop next door to the swimming pool. I'm sitting across from them in a booth as I scrape the last bite of my tiger ice cream from its cardboard bowl.

Rosie gazes at Warner with flushed cheeks, her ice cream a forgotten pile of melting pink goo in front of her. He pushes his shaggy brown hair out of his eyes, laughing at a silly joke she told about ghosts being bad liars (because you can see right through them, of course).

I grin and shake my head. For once, I'm relaxed around Warner. He's been on his best behaviour since we walked in. Not only did he pay for our desserts, but he carried them to the table for us too. If he keeps this up, I might even forgive him for ruining my painting.

I catch Rosie's eye, and she beams at me.

Warner leans back in the plastic bench seat and puts his arm across the back, behind Rosie. "How about this one. What's a ghost's favourite dessert?"

Rosie giggles and swats his arm. "I-scream, obviously."

Warner flashes her a wide-eyed smile, looking like he's about to bat his eyelashes. I wrinkle my nose. These two are so cute it's almost sickening.

Rosie clears her throat. "Anyways, Warner,

like I told you earlier, we have a few questions about your cousin. If you're still okay with that."

Warner shrugs. "Shoot."

"Okay, well, um . . ." Rosie begins. I can practically see the butterflies whirling in her head. "Did she maybe have a necklace? With a locket on it?"

Warner stiffens and frowns at her. "I don't know. Why?"

Rosie glances at me and swallows. "Well, we think we contacted her last night—"

"What?" Warner's brows shoot up, disappearing behind his long bangs. "What do you mean, contacted her? She's dead."

Rosie looks like a rabbit in a trap, ready to jump out of her skin. She runs her hands through her loose hair. "Well, Lavender's been seeing something, or somebody, hanging around her house. Her mom has a Ouija board—"

Warner barks a laugh. "You can't be serious, Kaur. Only crazy people believe in that stuff." He shoots me a dark look. "People like Lavender's mom. She's bonkers."

My spine hardens, and I narrow my eyes at him. "Excuse me? That's my mother you're talking about."

"You heard me. Your mom's loony." Warner slides out of the booth and stands over us. He points at me. "And so are you, Lavender, if you believe a word she says."

Rosie pushes her soggy bowl away from her. "Warner, please. Lavender lost her grandma's locket, and when we used the Ouija board, somebody who looks like Emma came through." She takes a deep breath. "She spelled the word locket."

Warner's face twists into a scowl, and his ears turn red.

"We thought you might know something about it." Rosie's voice is high and flustered. She stares at his angry expression and swallows. "Never mind. It's fine, Warner."

"It's not fine, Rosie." He glowers at her. His face is the colour of a ripe tomato. "You two need to mind your own business. I have no idea what locket you're talking about. You're both nuts."

He leans over, squashes his empty paper bowl, and flings it at Rosie. It hits her in the chest, leaving a brown stain on her pink t-shirt.

I gasp and whirl in my seat. "How dare you—"

"Shut it, nuts-o." Warner gives us one last

glare, then barges out of the ice cream shop. The chimes above the door tinkle as it swings shut.

My heart hammers in my chest. I grip the edge of the table with white knuckles. Did that seriously just happen?

I glance at Rosie, who's dabbing at her shirt with a napkin. She avoids my gaze, her eyes brimming with tears.

"Are you okay?" I lean across the table and grab her hand.

She jerks it away from me. "I'm fine. I'm sorry, Lavender. I guess we shouldn't have brought up Emma."

I stare at her, my stomach churning. "There's no excuse for him to act like that. He can't treat you that way."

Rosie takes a shaky breath and crumples

the napkin in her hand. "Emma only died a few months ago. We should have been more sensitive."

"No." I tilt my head. My heart hurts for my friend. "No, Rosie. That doesn't make it okay."

I pick up the scrunched bowl from the table and put it inside my empty one.

"Just let me talk to him." Rosie slides from the booth and glances down at her shirt. She tugs at it and frowns. "Can we talk later? I need to go home and change."

I blow through my lips and slide out from the table. After tossing the garbage into the trash can, I grab Rosie's hand and pull her in for a hug.

"He doesn't deserve you."

Rosie chokes back a sob, wraps an arm around my waist and returns the embrace. "I'll message you later."

With that, she pulls away from me and leaves the shop.

I grab a fresh napkin from the dispenser and give the table a quick wipe, cleaning the splattered ice cream from Warner's outburst. The thought of his scowl as he crushed the bowl pops into my mind. I throw the dirty napkin away and make a mental note to check in with Rosie tonight.

I silently beg the universe to make her see the light and ditch that jerk. We can deal with Emma ourselves. And Rosie definitely doesn't deserve a "friend" who screams and throws things at her. Nobody does.

I exit the shop and start walking towards home. My thoughts, already spinning in my head, turn to my grandmother. I brush my bare collarbone with my fingertips and sigh, disappointed the necklace isn't there and this isn't all merely a bad dream. Not only do I have a missing locket and a stalker ghost to deal with, now I'm even more worried about Rosie and Warner.

This is not the relaxing summer I had in mind.

CHAPTER TEN

"I could have sworn the 'W' that Emma spelled on the Ouija board was for Warner." Rosie sighs as we walk down the trail in the woods behind my house. She grabs at a tall piece of ryegrass and snaps off the end. A hand-held camera bounces off her chest, hanging from a strap around her neck.

After the ice cream shop incident, Rosie showed up at my house and offered to help me look for the necklace. She'd changed into a clean shirt, and in the basket of her bike she had a flashlight, an old camera, and a digital meat thermometer.

"What's all that for?" I had asked with a raised brow.

Rosie grinned sheepishly. "In case Emma's around."

"You planning to cook her?"

"A spiritual presence is often first identified by a shift in temperature." Rosie blushed. "It's the only temperature gauge I could find in our house."

"Of course."

I watch now as Rosie brandishes the thermometer in front of her. She presses the buttons and squints at the screen. "I'm not sure if this is working right. It's all over the place."

"That's because it's meant to be stuck in a pork loin," I reply, "not waved around in the air like a bubble wand."

Rosie rolls her eyes, then shakes the thermometer and presses another button.

I glance at the sky and frown. The sun has reached the top of the trees and it won't be long before it's dark. We'd been searching the forest all evening for that necklace and came up with nothing.

I flick on my flashlight to light the shadowed underbrush beneath the pine trees. A silver glint catches my eye. The locket!

I step off the trail and part the tall grass. A torn granola bar wrapper lays limply on the ground. The tear across the side is warped so it almost looks like the wrapper is laughing at me.

I bite back a frustrated cry.

"It's no use. We're never going to find it!" Tears threaten to spill from my eyes. I snatch up the garbage and shove it in my pocket, then sit cross legged on the trail. I bury my face in my hands. "I'm going to have to come clean to Mom. I can't believe I lost Grandma's necklace for good. It meant so much to her—to my mom. And me, too."

The worst part is, Mom isn't going to be angry. Instead, she's going to be disappointed—which is so much worse than mad. She might even cry. I'd way rather she shout or ground me. I groan and pound the forest floor with a balled fist.

Rosie comes over and sits next to me. She places her arm around my shoulders. "Don't give up yet. It has to be somewhere." She gazes at the ground and her voice softens. "That ghost was trying to help us, I'm sure of it. I wish Warner would have been nicer. He could have helped us."

I snort. "Warner's only nice when he's getting something out of it. He's such a jerk, Rosie."

Her face scrunches as if she's about to cry.

My chest tightens. "I'm sorry. But you deserve better—"

"I know." She looks at me, her eyes brimming with tears. "He's a bully. I don't know why I didn't see that before. He can be so much fun, but he gets so angry at the drop of a hat. I mean, he's been through so much—"

"It doesn't matter." I shake my head. "It stinks his cousin died, but it doesn't give him the right to be cruel to you or anybody else. You're the kindest, loyalist, best friend in the world and you deserve the same in return."

Rosie's lip quivers, and she glances away.

After a moment, she squeezes my shoulders. "Let's search a bit more before we give up. I'd hate to go home without the locket. Where were you when you first realized it was missing?"

"The well," I reply. "That old stone well. It's not much further."

Rosie's eyes widen. "The well? As in W?"

I wipe the tear from my cheek and stare at her. The planchette of the Ouija board snaps into my mind, pointing straight at the W on the board.

Rosie hops to her feet, grinning. "It has to be!"

I stand and brush the grass from the back of my shorts. "It's worth a shot. Let's go."

We trot down the trail under the growing shadows of the towering pine trees. The sun has almost disappeared behind them. I have my flashlight out, waving its beam across the ground, hoping for any sign of a silver shimmer.

Soon, we reach the old well. The circular, waist-high wall of stones looks ancient. In the dusky light I can see a thick layer of moss growing on one side. The grass around it is almost as tall as the well itself. I walk over to it and place my hand on the top.

I turn to Rosie, who's waving the thermometer in front of her. "I was right here when I realized it was gone. I was looking for Blot. He seems to like it here. This is where I usually find him when he escapes."

As if on cue, Blot leaps from the grass behind the well onto the stone wall. He pads over to me and rubs his shoulder on my arm.

"What are you doing here?" I shake my head and rub his ears affectionately. "Escaped again, you little devil."

Blot mews and bumps my hand with his head.

A sharp chill drops around us, and the hairs on my arms stand to attention.

"Lavender—" Rosie flicks her gaze from the thermometer to me. "The temperature's dropped. A lot."

There's a rustling noise in the bushes behind her. Blot lets out an angry yowl and jumps from the well. He dashes into the trees where the rustling came from, and an angry shout fills the air.

"You mangy little—"

Warner steps from the bushes, flailing his arms and kicking a leg behind him. Blot steps out calmly after him and pounces through the grass to my side.

Rosie lets out a surprised squeak.

I narrow my eyes and put my hands on my hips. "What are you doing here? Are you following us?"

Warner scowls and clenches his fists. "What do you mean, what am I doing out here? I can go wherever I want."

Rosie folds her arms across her chest. "You were following us, weren't you?"

Warner fixes her with a piercing glare. "I was going to your house to say sorry about our fight, but then I saw you leave with that weird stuff." He points to the camera around her neck. "I wanted to see what you were up to, and sure enough, you were headed to that freak's house." He jerks his head at me. "Ghost hunting—ridiculous."

He steps towards her and trips on a raised

tree root. He stumbles, and something silver tumbles from the side pocket of his shorts.

I shine the flashlight at it and clench my jaw. The locket!

Warner rights himself and snatches the necklace. He holds it up, dangling it from his finger.

Rosie gasps. "Warner!"

"You had it all this time!" I march over to him. "Give it back."

Warner swings the chain and catches the familiar heart pendant in his palm. "I found it the other night on the trail. The same night I saw you running through the woods like a maniac. It's mine now."

"It's not yours," I say through gritted teeth. "That's my family heirloom. You have no idea how much that means to my mother."

Warner sneers. "Finders keepers."

"That's not fair, Warner." Rosie grips the thermometer with white-knuckled fingers and points it at him. "Give it back. It's Lavender's. You know better!"

He looks her up and down, smirking. "I'll tell you what I know, and it's that ghosts aren't real. Lavender is a terrible influence on you, Rosie. Come with me and forget this mess." He knocks the thermometer out of Rosie's hand and grips her wrist. The thermometer hits the ground, the back pops off, and the batteries fly out from it.

Rosie's cheeks turn bright red. She wrenches her wrist from his grasp. "I'm not going anywhere with you! Enough is enough, give Lavender the necklace and get out of here."

Warner presses his lips together and scratches

his chin. "This necklace is sure causing a lot of trouble." He pushes me aside and stomps over to the well. "I think we'd all be better off without it." He looks me directly in the eye, gives me a cold smile, and tosses the necklace down the well.

My knees go weak. I gasp, a mixture of fury and devastation sweeping through me.

Rosie shrieks. "Warner! How could you? Get out of here. I never want to see you again!"

I dash to the well and lean over the edge. There's nothing but blackness. It's too deep, I can't see a thing. Tears flood my eyes.

Warner smirks and backs away from us. "Later, losers." He turns onto the trail and disappears.

Rosie shouts something after him, glaring at his retreating back, but I can't hear her over the ringing in my ears. How could I have let this happen? The necklace was right there!

Blot appears next to me and rubs along my legs. He meows. and I pick him up.

A cold wind rushes through the clearing, and a shiver runs up my spine. I clutch Blot tightly in my arms and turn to Rosie.

"Lavender? Are you okay?" Her face is etched with concern. She doesn't notice the flicker in the shadows behind her.

I grab her arm and pull her beside me, spinning her around.

"What are you—" Rosie's mouth gapes open. The grainy form of a young woman with black curtains for hair twitches into existence and lets out a terrifying shriek.

Rosie clutches my hand and gapes at the ghost.

I stand rooted to the spot, frozen in terror. Blot scratches my arms and leaps to the ground. He runs to the ghost's side. Emma, or whoever she is, bends over and runs her hand along his back in a strangely familiar manner.

She parts her hair and stares straight at me.

"Lavender."

My legs wobble. I recognize that voice in the breeze, the long black hair, and even the floor-length skirt.

It's definitely not Emma.

CHAPTER ELEVEN

I remember the picture on my mom's dresser of my young grandmother. Her smooth skin, full dark hair, and deep brown eyes match the ghost staring at me now.

Grandma! I choke back a sob.

She drifts forward, as if floating on the current of a stream, and stops directly in front of me. Blot pads along behind her, staring at his ghostly owner. My pulse throbs. That's why Blot keeps running out here—to see her.

My breath hitches. Up close, she's not scary

at all. Her face is soft, and the dark circles under her eyes make her look more tired than terrifying. She reaches for me as if to brush my hair behind my ear, but her translucent fingers go right through my purple strands without touching them.

I let out a sob. "I'm so sorry. I didn't mean to lose your necklace. Or to leave you all alone."

Grandma smiles kindly at me, revealing the familiar dimple in her left cheek. Her soft voice whispers in the wind. "It's okay, Lavender."

My insides warm, and the tension in my body eases. It's hard to explain, but she gives off an aura of peace and calm. My chest tingles. There I go again, thinking like Mom.

"But why are you still here? If you're not upset with me, then what's your unfinished business?"

I watch in disbelief as Grandma turns to Rosie and gives her a knowing grin. She pats at Rosie's arm, not actually touching her.

Rosie shivers and rubs her arm. "I think she's pleased with me."

Grandma claps her hands silently.

I nudge Rosie with my elbow. "You told off Warner."

Rosie lets out a giggle, and my grandmother raises her arms above her head in a silent cheer.

Her voice, even quieter now, floats through the air. "You're safe now."

I gape at her ghostly form. "You stayed for Rosie. You were worried about her."

Grandma nods, gazing at us as her form flickers. She shrugs, lifting her palms in the air. "She didn't need me, after all."

She cups her colourless hand around the side

of my face. It feels like a cool breeze against my cheek.

"I love you, Grandma." I choke out the words.

A white light shines around her, and her form begins to fade into it. "I love you too, Lavender. And you as well, Rosie."

With a wink, she disappears, leaving behind a soft light that dwindles out. Blot sits in the grass where she stood—or is it floated?—seconds ago, gazing upwards. He lets out a kitten-like mew.

A tear slides down my cheek.

"Lavender. . ." Grandma's voice whispers in my ear. The words are so quiet I can barely hear them. "Look in the well."

Rosie and I exchange glances.

"Did you hear that?" Rosie asks.

I nod, and we both rush to the side of the well. I shine my flashlight into the darkness, and a glimmer of silver catches my eye.

I gasp. The old stones on the well had warped with time, creating small ledges and tiny corners where a smooth wall had once been. The necklace hung precariously from a tip of one of the twisted stones. By some miracle, it dangled only a few feet from the edge.

I pass Rosie the flashlight, and she shines it onto the locket. She grabs the back of my shirt with her free hand. "Careful."

Gripping the edge of the well with one hand, I reach as far as I can with the other. I hold my breath, and my fingers brush against the silver chain. The necklace swings, and for a moment I'm afraid I've lost it. I grasp at it again and jerk it from the stone, then scramble backward away from the well with the locket in my hand.

Rosie lets out a whoop and punches the air.

"I got it!" Clumsily, I flip open the clasp to reveal the photo of my grandparents gazing out at me. For a split second, I swear my grandmother winks.

Blot appears at my side, mews, and rubs against my calf.

I put the necklace safely in my pocket, pick him up, and turn to Rosie. "Let's get home. Before I lose it again."

"I'm pretty sure it's safe now." Rosie picks up the battered thermometer and casts me a forlorn look. "This, on the other hand, is destroyed. The screen's cracked."

"I'm sorry, Rosie," I reply. "We'll replace it."

She sighs, shoves the broken device in her back pocket, and then shines the light on the trail. As we walk, with Blot safely clutched in my arms, she gives me a sideways glance. "So, did that actually happen? Did we see your grandma's ghost?"

My heart pounds as I think about the spiritual encounter. "I think we did."

A wide grin spreads across Rosie's face. "We should take your mom's Ouija board to my house and—"

"No." I raise my chin and hug Blot to my chest. Instead of squirming like usual, he purrs and rubs his head on my chin. "No way. No more paranormal stuff."

Her grin falls away. She darts her glance away from me and stares at the circle of light from her flashlight.

I let out a long, slow sigh. "Unless, of course, that ghost reaches out to you again. Then we'll have no choice but to see what it wants."

She skips ahead of me and calls over her shoulder, "We could start our own paranormal investigation business. Like that show—"

I groan. "Let's not get ahead of ourselves."

Soon, we see the lights of my house through the trees, and the path widens. I spot Mom's car in the driveway. We must have been out in the woods a lot longer than I thought.

As we get closer, I can see Mom's silhouette on the front porch, pacing back and forth.

"Lavender Azalea Raine," she calls out, her arms crossed. "Rosie Kaur. What are you two doing out in the woods this late? I was worried sick. Do your parents know you're here?"

Rosie waves back. "Yes, I told them I was sleeping over."

I let Blot down. He bolts up the porch stairs

and winds between Mom's legs. She bends down and scratches his back. Her voice softens. "Did Blot run away again?"

I run my hand through my hair and exchange glances with Rosie. "We've got a lot to tell you."

She straightens and takes in our serious faces. "Well, then I guess I should put the kettle on."

CHAPTER TWELVE

Over steaming mugs of peppermint tea on the kitchen table, Rosie and I tell Mom everything. Blot lays on the cushioned chair next to me, purring. The silver necklace sits in the middle of the table beside the tea pot, looking as shiny and perfect as ever.

Mom nods along with our story, frowning when I tell her about using the Ouija board, gasping when Rosie explains her argument with Warner, and raising her brows when we talk about Grandma's ghost. But she never interrupts.

Once we're finished, she regards us with a look that's half amused and half you're-grounded-forever. She spoons some more honey into her tea and swirls it around, gazing at her cup.

After a moment, she looks up. "So you're sure Grandma has crossed over to the other side, then?"

I glance at Rosie, who nods her head. "I'm pretty sure. She dissolved into a white light. And she seemed satisfied with what happened."

"According to that book you lent me," Rosie pipes in, "a white light is the passage to the next world."

Mom sets her teaspoon on the table. She sighs and gives us a wry look. "Well, that was quite the adventure. I'm glad you are both okay."

Heat creeps up my neck as I stare at my polka-dot mug. The steam from it swirls into the air. "I'm so sorry, Mom. I didn't mean to worry you. And I'm sorry about losing the necklace, too. You aren't angry?"

She raises a brow, but there's a small smile on her lips. "I'm disappointed that you lied to me, Lavender. But I understand why." She picks up the locket and flips it open. She gazes at the photo of her parents. "I'm not surprised Grandma felt compelled to help you, Rosie. And she always was eccentric. She probably thought playing poltergeist was fun."

Rosie's expression hardens. "She doesn't need to worry about me. Not now. I'm done with Warner."

"Thank goodness." I reach over and grasp

her hand. "We're too young to worry about romance, anyways."

Rosie rolls her eyes but squeezes me back. "I wasn't worried about romance."

"Sure you weren't."

Chuckling, Mom rises from the table. "All right girls, let's go pick a movie. Heaven knows you deserve some time to relax."

"You mean, Grandma knows?" I reply.

"Hmm. I suppose she does." Mom winks at me and leaves the kitchen. With a perky meow, Blot jumps from his chair and trails after her.

I stand from my seat, pick up my tea, and jerk my head toward the living room. "Coming, Rosie?"

Rosie nods and joins me at the kitchen exit. She pauses, catching my eye, and whispers, "Do you think we should ask your mom about borrowing the Ouija board again?"

I press my lips together. "Right now? Let's wait until this cools off." I bump her hip with mine. "Besides, my mom said they're dangerous. Sometimes they invite unwanted spirits."

Just as I finish speaking, the light above the table flickers—exactly how it did the night we contacted Grandma.

Rosie stares at me with wide eyes.

I burst into laughter and nudge her with my elbow. "It's just the wiring."

Rosie grins sheepishly and heads into the living room.

I glance over my shoulder. There's a human-shaped shadow looming above the potted cactus on the window sill.

"Coming, Lavender?" Mom calls from the

living room.

"I'll be right there."

Pursing my lips, I shake my head at the figure. Maybe Mom is right about using that Ouija board. Maybe we did open a door for an unwanted visitor. The form holds up a shadowed hand and wiggles its fingers in my direction. There doesn't seem to be anything menacing about it.

I should tell Mom and Rosie. But right now, I want to chill out. I snort a laugh and exit the kitchen.

My mom and best friend are seated on the couch. Mom is holding the remote, flipping through movies.

"How about Casper the Ghost?" I place my tea on the coffee table and flop down between them.

"I would think you'd be sick of ghosts by now." Rosie smirks.

I give her a sly smile. "I think we can handle one more."

Follow Lavender and Rosie's
next haunting adventure in
Lavender Raine and the Field of Screams!

The last thing Lavender Raine wants to see is another ghost, which is why she's ignoring the shadow lurking around her house. But her best friend, Rosie, is on a mission to prove they are real. When their classmates tease her for believing in the paranormal, Rosie is determined to capture a video of a ghost rumoured to haunt the local corn maze.

Lavender thinks the spooky story about the farm is made up. But when they enter the maze, weird things begin to happen. Broken flashlights, witchy laughter, that strange swishing noise in the corn—it's all in their imaginations, right? After getting lost in the dark field, a terrifying presence appears on the trail. Something sinister is stalking them, and it's up to the girls to figure out what it wants.

With some unexpected help, can Lavender and Rosie escape from the Field of Screams?

ABOUT THE AUTHOR

An avid reader and writer since she was a child, Jessica Renwick inspires with tales of adventures about friendship, courage, and being true to yourself. She is the author of the award-winning children's fantasy series, Starfell.

She enjoys a good cup of tea, gardening, her pets, consuming an entire novel in one sitting, and outdoor adventures. She resides in Alberta, Canada on a cozy urban homestead with her partner, fluffy monster dogs, four chickens, and an enchanted garden.

You can find her at www.jessicarenwickauthor.com, on Instagram @ jessicarenwickauthor, on Facebook, and on Goodreads.

Authors rely on word-of-mouth. An honest review on Amazon, Goodreads, or your choice of bookseller would be greatly appreciated. Just a few words can make a big difference.

Made in United States
Orlando, FL
26 November 2023

39557068R00075